by Eric Seltzer

illustrated by Tom Disbury

Ready-to-Read

Simon Spotlight

New York London Toronto Sydney New Delhi

For Kate Klimo and Cathy Goldsmith —E. S.

For Arwyn —T. D.

SIMON SPOTLIGHT
An imprint of Simon & Schuster Children's Publishing Division
1230 Avenue of the Americas, New York, New York 10020
This Simon Spotlight edition December 2022

Manufactured in the United States of America 1122 LAK
2 4 6 8 10 9 7 5 3 1
Library of Congress Cataloging-in-Publication Data
Names: Seltzer, Eric, author. | Tinn-Disbury, Tom, illustrator. Title: Bookstore bunnies / by Eric Seltzer ; illustrated by Tom Disbury. Description: New York : Simon Spotlight, 2022. | Series: Ready-to-read. Pre-level 1 | Audience: Ages 3–5 | Audience: Grades K-1 | Summary: "Bunnies have a bookstore in this Pre-Level 1 Ready-to-Read by Eric Seltzer and Tom Disbury! What is more fun than bunnies reading? Reading about bunnies reading! Bookstore bunnies check the time. Their store opens right at nine. Bookstore bunnies have every book. Come inside and take a look!"—Provided by publisher. Identifiers: LCCN 2022012209 (print) | LCCN 2022012210 (ebook) | ISBN 9781665927925 (paperback) | ISBN 9781665927932 (hardcover) | ISBN 9781665927949 (ebook) Subjects: CYAC: Stories in rhyme. | Rabbits—Fiction. | Animals—Fiction. | Bookstores—Fiction. Classification: LCC PZ8.3.S4665 Bo 2022 (print) | LCC PZ8.3.S4665 (ebook) | DDC [E]—dc23 LC record available at https://lccn.loc.gov/2022012209LC ebook record available at https://lccn.loc.gov/2022012210
ISBN 978-1-6659-2793-2 (hc)
ISBN 978-1-6659-2792-5 (pbk)
ISBN 978-1-6659-2794-9 (ebook)

Bookstore bunnies
open at nine.

Skunk and Gator
both wait in line.

BUY MORE BOOKS
READ MORE BOOKS
BOOKS ARE THE BEST
I am here to help

Cat wants a book
of ABCs.

Dog wants a book
on ticks and fleas.

Owl wants a book
on being wise.

Frog wants a book
on catching flies.

CATCHING FLIES
and
BAKING PIES

Mouse wants a book
about grilled cheese.

GRILLED
EXPECTATIONS
WAR
and
CHEESE

Bear wants a book

on saying "please."

Skunk wants a book from the highest shelf.

Bookstore bunnies
hop up to help.

Then story hour begins at four.

Chicks and ducks
rush through the door.

Chicks and ducks
sit in each row.

The book is full
of things that go.

“We love that book!”
quack the ducks.

Chicks love to learn about big trucks!

TRUCK
DUMP TRUCK

Now it is time
to end the day.

Bookstore bunnies
put books away.

Bookstore bunnies
close the front door.

Soon they all will
read some more!